Pitz: A Tale Of Urban Terror

Acknowledgment

CEO……..………Darrell King

COO……………Elbert Jones Jr.

Graphics………Muhammad Asad

asadxeo@gmail.com

Website………..…… jrempires.com

Chapter 1

By 2007 the North King Street wasn't a peaceful Street anymore. As the night fell, all the drug addicts would surround it in a hope that someone would throw some ballot or at least some back breakers. The infamous "Triple Double Kennels" owned by the disgraced and incarcerated NBA star point guard Mario Mixx of the Atlanta Hawks was located there. Mario and his drug dealing cronies took over a former nightclub with the purpose of organizing illegal dog fights, which they successfully did. Every night they would have wild parties and ferocious dog fights. The local authorities seemed to be "blinded", and there was no way they would have even tried to do anything about it.

In their fights, the "Triple Double Kennels" used mostly pit bull terriers and other mixed breeds, mostly dangerous feral dogs, which were taken care by Joe and Kyle, the only two persons Mario could really trust.

It was 2 a.m. and Mario was having a drink while bragging about his last fight.

"Mah white pit-bull was fighting so good, nigga! Lil' John grabbed that little piece of shit by the neck and fucking ripped him apart!"

Kyle his right hand was trying to tell him about his new white boy who bragged around about how good his dogs are.

"Yeah, I saw that, savage! But you should really've seen this white boy's dogs! You should've seen him talking about his dogs, like… he thinks he's so good, he said he could beat yo ass in a fight."

"What the fuck, nigga? You really think I could get my ass beaten by a white boy?! Hell no, that shit ain't gonna happen!"

"But Mario! I saw he has really good dogs! And you could get your hands on them if he loses!"

"If?????!" Mario was getting mad at the thought that he could ever lose, especially to a white boy.

"I'm sure he's gonna lose, ain't nobody got better dogs than yours, Mario." Joe said as he came in overhearing the conversation.

"That's what I'm thinkin'! Have you seen 'em?"

"No, but Kyle says they're good, so I don't know, man."

Mario didn't know what to do but in the end he had to accept the proposal, because he was really tempted by the thought of adding a few new dog to his pack. "Know what, nigga? I want him here tomorrow, at midnight, I want him to grab his best dogs if he thinks he can beat me and Lil' John will take care of the rest."

Lil Jon was Mario's best dog and there was no way any other dog could beat him. The giant white pit-bull had the biggest fangs any of the "Triple Double Kennels" members has ever seen, so Mario was pretty confident about winning the fight.

"We gonna see what the white boy can do…"

"You not gonna be disappointed, Mario, I know that." Kyle reassured him one more time before leaving. Mario sat back on his chair and finished his beer. He started to get really curious about this guy Kyle told him about, and he certainly could not wait for the next day to come.

"But why would a white boy risk coming to a black neighborhood for a dog fight only?" Mario asked looking at Joe.

"I don't know, man, maybe he thinks he can win, or somethin'"

"Now that's what worries me, he has to have some plan."

"Common, man, he's just a white boy, what could he be up to other than ready to lose?"

Chapter 2

"You better be right Kyle, you better be right." were the last words Mario said before entering the fight room with Lil Jon. He was not worried about this white boy, but he certainly was wondering what he looks like because he hasn't seen him before, and he has only heard Kyle talk about him. Mario entered the fight room while a huge hoard of dog fight lovers were cheering on him.

"Mario! Mario! Mario!" they were yelling while the pit bull

barks were accompanying their loud voices. Mario was extremely surprised when instead of the skinny white boy he has imagined, he saw a massive guy with an even bigger pit-bull terrier. It was the first time Mario actually worried for Lil' John and even considered backing up from the fight.

"Kyle?!" Mario looked towards his right, where he usually saw Kyle before every dog fight, but the good old friend was nowhere to be found. It was then when Mario realized there was something wrong. Something just didn't add up. And it was then when he realized the white boy was, in fact, Chris Torrow, known as one of the very few white drug dealers, that even some gangsters from the black neighborhood feared.

"You look pale." Chris said grinning at Mario. "Are you scared perhaps?"

But Mario wasn't scared, he was just really pissed off. He knew Kyle didn't just bring in a white boy, he brought in his once rival, Chris Torrow, his white competition, and he didn't like that. And, judging again by his dog, in fact, there was nothing he should have worried about, hence Lil' John has won over pit-bulls bigger than the one Chris has brought in the ring.

"Shall we fight" Chris grinned.

"Be my guest." Marion answered coldly, yet confident.

Cherry took the mic and stepped inside the ring. She was the girl that always made the introductions before each fight. No one really know her name, but they called her cherry because she was wearing a sparkly red bikini, and red boots whenever she stepped into the ring. She would usually name the pit-bulls fighting, their previous achievements and the owners. Once she was done with that, she would take off her top and throw it in the air while everyone cheered. Once the top hit the ground, the owners would free the dogs from their leashes and let the fight begin.

"So tonight we're havin' here the well-known, aggressively mad and ready to kill – Lil' John!!!!"

and she turned towards the dog who's mouth was foaming while growling at the other pit-bull. "We all know what a good boy he is, right?!" and she smiled at the crowd while they shouted in agreement. "Can we hear some cheering?" and everyone started shouting "Lil' John! Lil' John! Lil' John!"

Cherry turned towards the opponent dog "And here we have a new doggie, what you call him again?" she looked at Chris while the crowed started laughing.

"Shady." Chris answered.

"Shady! The grey puppy!" she coughed and continued "The grey, fierce terrier, I mean!" and she proceeded laughing as the crowd laughed too at Chris being humiliated. Someone close to Chris shouted "That's what you get with if you wanna fuck with the hood!"

"As for the owners! We have heeere Mario!!!! Cheers, people!" and everyone cheered again, shouting Mario's name. Mario couldn't help but smile, the crowd loved him and his dog, and he knew it. Then Cherry proceeded introducing Chris Torrow, who, despite being who he was, the hoard didn't cheer for.

"Shall the fight begin!?" Cherry made a pirouette in the middle of the ring while pulling off her top and raising her arm into the air.

"Yeaaaaahhh!!!!" everyone shouted. Cherry threw her top into the air, and once it hit the ground, both Mario and Chris freed their pit-bulls.

"Get'im, boy! Get'im!!" Mario encouraged his pit-bull.

"Jump, Shady!" Chris shouted, but he seemed rather chill, while Mario was totally into bucking Lil' John up.

Lil' John backed down a bit, and while Shady jumped at him, he slithered under him and grabbed him by the neck, stabbing the terrier with his fangs. The hoard cheered in amusement.

"Come on, Shady! Jump!"

"Ahahahahahaha" the entire crown burst into laughter.

"Yo, whitey, you gonna tell yo god to jump when he's being

trashed by Lil' John?!" someone yelled. The only one not laughing was Marion. He knew something had to be wrong. Why would Chris be so calm about his dog being bit? There must have been something wrong, and Marion knew it.

Chris' dog managed to free himself and backed down a bit, while Lil' John started muddying.

"Go get 'im boy!" Mario yelled, and Lil' John threw himself on Shady, this time biting the opponent's face, only more mellow this time. Chris began to grin. Mario got worried. Lil' John backed down and started to spin in dizziness around the place, while Shady jumped at him and started tearing the white pit-bull apart. Mario couldn't believe his eyes. The next thing he remembered was Cherry announcing Shady and Chris as the winners, while Lil' John lied down all mutilated, all covered in dark red blood.

"He's been sedated…" Marion whispered to himself in shock. "He's been sedated!!!" he shouted out loud, and the whole crowd silenced. "This fuckin' white cunt sedated my dog!!!"

"Hold up! We all saw your dog coward out and give up fighting!" Chris wickedly said, and some voices in the crowd silently agreed.

"He fuckin' sedated my dog! Lil' John doesn't give up! You fuckin' killed 'im!!"

"Mario, calm down, he's not alone…" Joe whispered as he grabbed Mario by his left arm. "We gonn' take care of him later, let him go now…"

"Kyle is in it…" Mario looked at Joe with rage.

"He's in it, I saw two of the white boy's men leave the club with him…"

"That nigga gonn' pay for Lil' John…" Mario kneeled and grabbed his bleeding dead dog into his arms. If there was anything Mario really cared about, that was his white dog, Lil' John, and it torn him inside to see his favorite fighter die.

Chapter 3

Nobody ever messed with Mario before and nobody ever thought of doing it because everybody knew you don't fuck with him, so everyone also knew Chris doesn't have any more days to leave. Mario obviously ordered a few of his men to organize a shooting at Chris Torrow's place and the next day they found his dead body.

"That what white shit deserve if they fuck with the hood." Mario finally said after Joe confirmed Chris is dead. However, there was Joshua still, Chris Torrow's brother, and he decided to seek revenge. A few nights after his brother was found dead, he came to the dog fight club and asked to speak with Mario.

"Yo, whitey, where you think you're goin'?" one of the guards stopped him as he tried to enter the club.

"I want to talk to Mario, Mario Mixx."

"He waitin' for ya?"

"No, he's not. He doesn't know I'm coming, but I'm here peacefully."

"Yo name?"

"Joshua Torrow."

The guard recognized the name, everyone knew Chris Torrow killed Mario's best dog, but he had to let him know this guy came to talk to him anyway.

"Let'im in. If he doesn't leave the club in 20 minutes, come in an' shoot him."

Joshua entered the club and as soon as he saw Mario, he tried to apologize.

"Look, man, I know what Chris did, I am sorry, but I hear he had some issues with you in the past, and I suppose he had his reasons. Now he's my brother and I would normally seek vengeance. But I won't. Not this time. I have nothing against you, so I would rather fall on an agreement with you. I will take my brother's place and I will continue his business but I don't want you or any of your men messing with me."

Mario was not impressed with his offer. Not at all. And even if he had enough money, even if he had enough women and a lot of other good fight dogs, the fact that a white boy killed his favorite dog made him really angry, and there was no way he would agree to this one. He decided however to give him a chance because after all he killed Chris and he killed Shady.

"Look" Mario said "I ain't gonna try to kill you, and I ain't makin' any agreement with you, but Imma keep it real, and I ain't gonna haunt you."

"Man, I understand you, I know what it's like to lose your best friend."

At this point Mario wasn't sure whether Joshua was dumb or just playing stupid.

"Yeah." He agreed shaking his head towards Joe, signaling that they gotta get rid of this one.

What Mario did not know was that in the meantime, Joshua's men killed his guards, shoot some of the dogs, and freed the other ones. When Mario found out, Joshua was long gone, and there nothing else left to do than organize a new mass shooting and kill every single one related to the white brothers.

"Ain't no crackhead gonn' destroy my fight club. Those shits gonna pay."

He grabbed Joe and a few other men, went to Joshua's place the same night, and shoot everyone in the house, including wife and kids. The he poured gasoline all over the place and set it on fire.

A few days later he left Hampton as the police started to look into the 'incident', as they called it. The only thing left on Mario

Mixx was now his name, and rumors that he had a dog fight club on the North King Street in Hampton. Nobody even cared anymore about the drug addicts roaming the street at night, as they didn't have who to blame for it anymore, and when people don't have someone to blame, they forget about it.

Chapter 4

It's been over a month since anyone has last mentioned anything about the "burning house incident". People tend to forget quickly things that are not directly related to them, therefore nobody talked anymore about Mario Mixx, the dog fight club, or about the Torrow family. The only folks still wondering about it where the Hood's Brothers, who knew something simply didn't add up. They knew about the dog fights as they themselves visited the place quite a few times, as part of the crowd. They knew Mario Mixx wasn't someone who would simply give up on his source of money, as a lot of bets washed lots of money through that club, and something certainly must have happened, 'cause you can't simply get vanished overnight along with 2 pit-bull terriers. The Hood's Brothers were best known for beating all those gangster-wannabe asses when they tried to mess with the neighborhood's girls or children. Being a group of homeboys who would venture to help anyone who needed it, they would usually worry about things the other people wouldn't even acknowledge, and, unfortunately they weren't even surprised when Frank, their so called boss, told them what he heard on the news. The local authorities have announced they have found 2 mutilated bodies somewhere near the Hampton Roads Beltway.

"I fuckin' knew it!" said Frank "I've been knowin' Mario for too long as to know he ain't simply leavin'. We are gonna have to do somethin' about it if things get worse."

"But, boss, what can we do about it? We don't even know what happened to those niggas."

"I am pretty sure Mario's dogs are behind all this. Only thing is right now I don't know how or why would he do such a thing."

"Wait, you mean Mario freed his dogs?"

"I don't know. Maybe or maybe not, but I don't think he'd do this. That why I am quite worried.

"So we gonna do shit about it?" one of the homies asked.

"No. Not yet. But soon we're gonna have to take the matters in our own hands if the police doesn't do its job as expected. And we already know that our local officers are dumb as fuck." Frank was a smart guy and if he said something it could only mean that he knows what he is talking about. Everyone knew that. And no one would have ever dared to doubt his words.

"I guess he is right." Martin, one of the homies said.

"He gotta be right." Another one confirmed.

What was really interesting is the fact that even the people from the hood relied more on Frank's gang, rather than all the police officers regarding the two mutilated bodies discovered. However, no one knew, nor had the slightest idea that behind the mutilated bodies was a fierce pack of roving feral dogs that were ready to kill whoever stood in front of them.

"We are really scared!" Said one of the people from the neighborhood when the local news program organized an interview regarding the mutilated bodies.

"But what do you think? Who, or what is behind all this?" The interviewer asked for the sake of talking.

"I don't know. Maybe some wild animals. Or maybe even some people that we can't even call people if that's the case."

Even if it was clear enough that the mutilated bodies were caused by some sort of wild creature, people still where making up things about it, or at least didn't want to acknowledge the fact that behind the tragedy were some animals. A week later three more bodies were found.

The bodies were of a woman and her 2 children, whom she were probably walking to the daycare center located at the South Boxwood Street intersection with the Hampton Roads Beltway, as the authorities suspected. The girl and the boy, brother and sister were found completely torn, with their guts all over the place and mutilated skulls, while the woman's abdomen muscles were still twitching even if she was long dead. It was a sign the bodies have been killed recently, and the police decided it was time to track the culprits. Little knew they it was in vain.

A few more weeks past and the number of deaths has increased significantly.

"The police has publicly announced the culprits in the 12 mutilated bodies have been found, and they are a pack of pit-bulls that have allegedly escaped form a former illegal dog fighting club." The news announced as Frank turned the TV on.

"We are trying our best in order to catch the wild pack, and for now we ask you to stay home, in the safety of your own places, rather than adventure outside. We suggest you make supplies of food and reduce the time out at the minimum possible." An office representative said. They were just trying to calm the neighborhood, but it was already clear as day that things have gotten out of control. Besides, Frank knew how the local police department worked. No matter how bad the things were, all the police did was trying to assure people that everything was under control, when in reality, it has never been.

"Katie? You ready?" he shouted looking upstairs.

"Commin' in a second!" his little sister yelled. "I'm brushing my teeth!"

"Didn't I tell ya to do it earlier?"

"But Frank…"

Katie was the best thing he had. Everything he cared about was compressed in that little human he took care of, especially since he moved here. If there was anything Frank was ready to fight for, that was his sister and The Hood's Brothers.

"Take care" he said as he left his little sister in front of the Hampton Daycare Center. Since the mutilated bodies have been found, he walked her there, and back home, every single day, and no exceptions were ever made. Turning to the teacher, Frank made sure to let her know she could always call if something bad were to happen.

"Just call me, OK? Imma be here in a minute. If somethin', just call me."

"OK, Frank, I will call you, but I don't think there is any reason to worry, as long as you walk little Katie here and back home, everything is going to be alright."

Even if the teacher's voice was reassuring, Frank knew better he couldn't rely on that. He had a bad feeling.

As soon as he jumped in his car, he got a call from Martin, his homie.

"Yeah?" he answered while starting the car.

"Fuck, Frank! I'm caught between the pack of dogs!!! You gotta do something'!"

"What?! Where you at?! You in yo car?!"

"Ye, an' I'm on Boxwood, under the bridge… My car broke down, and the dogs are all on it! Fuck, nigga, they trynna break my windows!!"

Martin was clearly scared, and Frank headed towards him right away.

"Don't worry, Martin, we gonna get you outta there!"

"Be fast, nigga, I don't wanna die!" Martin cried terrifyingly, and then he hung up. He kept trying to turn the car engine on, but it just wouldn't work. A massive brown pit-bull jumped on the front window of the car and started hitting with its head against it.

"Fuck, fuck, fuck!!!!"

The horrendous pit-bull kept hitting with its head in the window and the glass started crippling.

"Fuck! Fuck! No!!" Martin cried in despair, frantically searching for his gun. He grabbed it and pointed it at the dog shouting, ready to shoot. As the pit-bull hit the window one more time, the glass broke, and he shot the dog. The nightmare was not over though, the other ferocious dogs jumped in to massacre Marion, who, after a few bullets was powerless. One of the dog jumped and stabbed its fangs in Martin's face, causing him to shout in despair and hit the dog however he could, but the dog was devouring his face, while another one jumped on his legs and put the fans in his right arm. Soon all the pack was roaming around the car, smelling the fresh blood of the newly mutilated body.

Frank called to the other Hood brothers and told them were Martin is, and in 10 minutes they were there. Too late though, for 10 minutes was more then enough for the dogs to eat Martin alive. The dogs were still there when the rest of the Hood's Brothers got there. They didn't hesitate a second, and started shooting in the dogs, but the pit-bulls weren't only fast and ferocious, but also extremely smart. They sensed the danger, and instead of attacking, they run away, leaving behind 2 of the weakest dogs that got shot by the Hood's bullets.

Tony started crying, he was Martin's brother, they were all brothers in a way, hood brothers, but Martin was his blood-brother, and blood was above anything even for them. He sworn he's gonna kill those dog, he sworn he's gonna make everyone pay for his brother, and the scene itself was terrifying, but Frank and the other homies knew they can't let him go anywhere. Not like that, at least. They knew that they had to do something about it though, and they needed do to it fast.

Later the same day, after the new death has been reported and the police circled the place once more, without arriving to any solution, The Hood's Brothers started to make a plan about capturing the dogs, or, at least, killing them.

"We have to get to them somehow…" Tony said.

"Or we could wait for them to come to us." Frank's face suddenly lightened. "They've been seen mostly around The Hampton Roads Beltway, and now Boxwood Street."

Things were starting to get clear.

"It means those fuckers are hidin' in the nearby woods."

"Do we have enough guns?" someone wondered.

"We gonna run outta guns, we gonna fight those bitches with

baseball bats. They gonna eat the baseball bats, we gonn' fight 'em with our own bare hands! We gotta free the hood from this terror!" Frank was more determined than ever.

"That's right, man, people are countin' on us…"

Chapter 5

They spent an entire week making the perfect plan, and it was not about killing the dogs. If there was a way to solve the problem while keeping the ferocious dogs alive, they had to do it. Frank, being the smartest one of the all, came up with a brilliant idea.

"Know what we gonn' do? We gonna feed those puppies! We gonna feed them sedatives."

"We gonn' what?"

"Listen up. We gonn' get some meat for those beasts, and use sedatives. If everything work fine, they gonna fall asleep, then we get the chance to tie them up and get rid of them."

"Tie them? Why? What for, Frank? We ain't gonna shoot them?"

"Nah, man, I'd rather we get them to some animal shelter, they know better."

"They killed my brother, Frank!" Tony got angry.

"Tony, brother, listen, we can't just... I understand you, but..."

"No, you fuckin' don't, nigga!" and he left slamming the door.

"He gonn' be back. He gonn' be back!" Frank pointed at the door while looking at the other homies.

It wasn't one of the best moments, but they had to try stick to their plan. So they did it. Two of the Hood's Brothers were in charge with bringing the meat and sedatives, while the rest had to make sure they still had guns and baseball bats on them. They were supposed to meet under the

Hampton Roads Beltway at 8 pm, right after Frank brought Katie home.

"Frank, we're there. Where you at?" one of the guys called him.

"I'm on my way, gonn' be there in 20 minutes. Everything fine?"

"Yeah, no dogs yet."

While driving towards the place they were supposed to meet, Frank had no idea what was about to happen. The pack of ferocious dogs blocked the street. There were 15 huge dogs, showing off their sharp fangs covered in foam only making the picture more mortifying. Frank did not get scared or panicked, he continued to drive, but the dogs didn't seem to get intimidated, as they were running towards the car's direction. Now Frank got a better idea, instead of trashing the dogs and scare them off, he would lure them towards the place where his homies where. All he had to do as to make sure he doesn't hit nay of the dogs, so that they would not get scared away. And he did just that, he slowed down and carefully drove through the crazy dogs that kept barking and grinning at him. Two of the beasts jumped on the front car window, and Frank saw it coming, so he speeded up, letting the pit-bulls roll on the ground. As he sped up, the fierce and wild pack of wild beasts took after him. He called the guys.

"Niggas, you ready? Imma get you somethin' when I get there!" Frank sounded pretty excited.

"Everythin' good, Frank?"

"Yeah, get yo asses in the cars, I'm bringin' the puppies after me. Is the meat ready?"

"Yes, boss, it is, but we not ready, we saw what those bastards can do."

"It gonna be fine, yo!" and he hung up.

By half past 8, the brothers could hear the beasts barking as they raced after Frank's car. It was a wild picture.

"Holly crap..." one of the guys let out.

"We're fucked up, man..."

"Hello, there, niggas!" Frank yelled with a huge grin on his face as he lowered his right car window.

"Dis nigga's crazy…"

Frank circled the place a few times, and then parked next to the other 3 cars.

"What's up?!" and he laughed.

"You crazy, man…"

"Nah, we just gotta wait till they gonn' eat the meat, and we're cool."

And then they waited. An hour past, but the fierce pack had no intention to even smell the meat. The wild beast were way smarter than anticipated. Al they did was circle the cars and jump on their window trying to hit the glass in hope to break it, just like they previously did with Martin. It was then when the entire gang realized they just might have messed up everything.

"Man, we fucked up…" one of them said. Frank shook his head.

"Looks like we gonna have to leave, niggas. Gotta shoot some mofos and make sure they don't follow us to the hood."

"And how we gonn' do that? They followed you for 20 minutes, no?"

"They did, yeah, but… there must be a way…"

Suddenly one of them cried. "Fuck! Fuck! They're breaking my glass! For fuck's sake! Do somethin'!!"

Frank took the gun and shoot on of the dogs right through his window glass, and started the engine. "We getting' outta here!We gonna drive on the Hampton Roads Beltway till we getting' as far as possible form our hood, and there, we lure them in the woods, and then we can shoot as we please!"

"Fuck! Fuckin' hate dogs!" someone shouted while starting the engine. They successfully drove along Hampton Roads, until they were finally in the middle of the wilderness, while the ferocious pack followed them barking and foaming around their fangs like they had rabies. There they took on shooting the dogs.

"Fuckin' shoot everythin', nigga!"

"Oh fuck! It's breaking in! The fucker is almost inside my car!"

"Shoot him, homie! Shoot 'im!"

"Ain't got no more bullets! Fuck!"

Frank got really pissed, h opened the right door of the car and yelled at the dog trying to mutilate his homie.

"Come at me, fucker!" he tried getting the dog mad, and that was enough, the beast focused on him, and while he tried to jump at him, Frank shoot a bulled straight into his head. At this point, the other dogs, seeing the fallen pit-bull, retreated into the woods yelping and bleeding.

"Fuck! Fuck! Fuck!"

"Yeah, that was close…" Frank breathed relived.

"I'm afraid shooting is the only way we gonn' get rid of them, Frank."

"I know, nigga, I know, we gotta do somethin', there must be a way, but now we gotta go home, I'm tired as fuck."

"I feel you, brother, I feel you."

And they left.

Chapter 6

"Frank?"

"Yes, baby girl?"

"Today I heard the teacher talk to a mom. And I'm scared."

"What did she say, Katie?"

"She said they found a new dead body, Frank…"

"It's ok, honey, ain't nobody gotta hurt you."

"But Frank… it was Stacy, my best friend…" and the little girl started crying. Frank reached to hug her.

"I'm sorry, Katie, but that's not gonna happen to you, I'm coming for you every day."

"Stacy's brother came after her every day, Frank, and now he's gone, too."

"He dead?"

"I don't know, they didn't find him…"

"Shhh, Katie, don't cry, it's gonn' be fine, you'll see."

"But I'm scared, Frank, I'm afraid. What if they hunt you down, too? Like they did with

Stacy's brother? Huh? What then?"

"You don't have to worry, ain't no dog stronger then your brother, honey." And he hugged her tighter.

"Your brother's gonna protect ya, OK? Imma kick those dog asses and they'll come say sorry for scaring this little girl, OK?" Katie managed to giggle, and she couldn't feel any safer than this.

"Now we gotta take you to daycare, did you brush your teeth?"

"I diiid." She finally smiled.

Frank took her backpack, as always, opened her door, and drove to the daycare. He drove for a good 30 minutes when he noticed some movement far ahead on the road.

"What the… honey, hold tight!" as he swiftly turned around and headed towards home.

"Ain't we going to the daycare, Frank?"

"Not today, sweetheart. You gonna stay home and watch SpongeBob, OK?"

"SpongeBob? Yay! Are you gonna watch with me, Frank?!" the little girl got really excited.

"Maybe a bit later, Frank gotta solve something first."

Little Katie had no idea what scared Frank so much, that he turned around, in fact, she though the only reason why he turned around was the fact that he decided to be a good brother and let her watch cartoons for a whole day, sparing her the pain of the daycare. She didn't like ti very much there, especially since the dogs got her best friend Stacy.

Frank took the girl home, turned on the cartoons channel and told Katie to not go anywhere for any reason.

"If your tummy hurts and you want to eat, grab some milk and cereals."

"Really?!" Katie was excited and surprised at the same time. IT was a strange thing for Frank to allow her eat cereals during the day.

Then he left, but not before locking the door form the outside. On his way to the car he called his homies.

"Yo, niggas, call everyone, we gotta meet at our place in 10."

"Somethin' wrong, Frank?"

"Just... do it. I got a very bad feeling." And he knew what he was saying. Not late after, he was at the loft where he and his guys usually met. Everyone was there except Shawn, one of the brothers.

"Where Shawn?"

"He said he meets Tony and they come here both."

"Oh, Tony, knew he'd be back." Frank didn't show any emotion, but he was happy, he's known him for his entire life, and he didn't like the fact that he was mad at him.

"Why you called us?"

"The daycare... I'm afraid the dogs are heading there."

"You sure?"

"I saw them while I was taking Katie there. They were running in the center's direction. I took Katie home, don't wanna risk, but I'm afraid those fuckers are aiming for the daycare center."

"The police ain't gonna do nothin' even if someone informs them."

"Yeah, that's why I called you, niggas. We gotta do something. And we gotta do it for good this time."

"What if the dogs ain't even there?"

"What if I'm right?"

"Yea, we better head there."

The Hood's Brothers were now prepared better than ever. They agreed to shoot every single beast once they get there, and get rid of them once and for all. Frank was about to say something when his phone rung.

"Hello?"

"Frank? Is this Katie's brother?!"

"Miss Smith? Everythin' fine?!"

"No…" – the crying teacher said scared – "we got surrounded, the pit-bulls are here… we called the police and they helped out the first 2 floors, but they said they can't do anything about the 3rd one, the children are scared, they got inside the building… Help us!"

"Oh, fuck…" one of the homies whispered.

"Listen up, Miss, don't panic! Take all the children and get all together in the safest room! Can you do that?!" the teacher wasn't answering. "Miss Smith?! Are you there?!"

"Yes… we are all together, but we can't leave, the dogs are everywhere. I am afraid, Frank!"

"Now calm down, what is the exact room you and the children are in? We're coming there now!" and he signaled to the brothers that they're going.

"It's the last room on the left..." the teacher cried.

"We gonna be there in a second. Don't move! And most important, try to keep silent! Don't let the dogs know you are there!"

"We are so scared, please help us..."

"We will help you, miss, we ain't lettin' you there. Now, make sure no one leaves the room under any circumstances, is that clear?!" and he assured her once more that everything is gonna be fine as he got in the car.

"Miss, when we get there, there might be shootings, take care of the children, and tell them not to be afraid!"

"OK, thank you so much, Frank…" the teacher kept crying.

"Now, I'm gonna hung up, but we gonna be there soon. Stay strong, miss!"

And after saying some more encouraging words, he hung up the phone.

"Things are fucked up, man, I knew it! Fuckin' cops! Doin'

nothing since the system was formed!"

"Calm down, Frank, we gonna win this fight."

"Of course, nigga, we must, there are children in there, an' those fuckers say they can't get to the 3rd floor?! Well, fuck you! We gonna get there!"

Not long after they were in front of the daycare center. There were two huge pit-bulls roaming around the building, and no trace of police.

"The fuckin' fuck is dis…"

"I know, we gotta really do it all alone." Frank said. "Now, the center has 3 entrances, John and Shawn, you are going through the back, Ryan and Scot through the left entrance, see that one there? Tony, Michael, and I are going through the main one."

Everyone agreed without saying a word.

"You niggas better watch your asses… Now, we know the room where the children and Miss Smith are hiding is the last on the left, the 3rd floor, right? We gotta get there in not more than 30 minutes. Make sure you shoot every fucker you see nice and clean. Don't waste bullets, understood?!"

"Yes, boss."

"And keep that fuckin' baseball bat on you, niggas, you gotta watch your own asses. Now we gonna meet there, and keep count of the dogs you shootin', last time we saw the pack there was a total of 15 beasts, and I bet they ain't less now."

"We goin' in?"

"We goin' in..." Frank finally said charging his gun and shooting one of the two dogs. The other dog started to run towards him, but Tony managed to shoot him before Frank even aimed at him.

"Good shot, I'm glad you're back." He said eyeing Tony. Tony shook his head in approval.

The gang split as planned: John and Shawn through the back, Ryan and Scot through the left entrance, while Tony, Michael, and Frank himself took the main one.

Tony, Michael and Frank were the first ones to enter the building. As soon as they got in, they noticed another dog smelling the corridor.

"You shoot 'im..." Frank whispered at Michael who had better aim.

As he shot the children got scared.

"They're here!" Miss Smith cheered! "The good boys are here, and they are going to save us, kids!" she exclaimed with tears in her eyes. The children were scared as hell, but the good news, and the idea of some badass gang fighting with the fierce pack of dogs excited them.

"Are they like some heroes?" one of the children asked with tears on his cheeks.

"Yes, Brandon, they are like heroes, and they are gonna take us out of here." She tried to calm all the children, when another shot was heard.

This time it was Shawn who shoot one of the dogs, still at the first floor.

"Damn, that was one good shot…" John whispered at Shawn.

"Thanks, bro, I'll leave the next one to you." And he winked.

Suddenly some barks were heard from the end of the 1st floor's corridor.

Ryan and Scot had the bad luck of stumbling upon three dogs at once as soon as they got inside the building.

"Shoot 'em, Scot!"

"Fuck! There's three of them!!"

Five shots were heard. Scot missed one bullet, but the beast were put to sleep now.

"That was easy..." Ryan grinned after he relaxed a bit form the tension.

"Yeah, wasn't that easy when you first saw it, now was it?" Scot laughed back at him.

"At least I didn't waste no bullet." Shawn mocked him back.

"Yeah, keep blabberin'."

And they kept walking along the corridor.

"Psst!" Michael whispered from the other side of the corridor. "We here already, we goin' up…"

"All clear?"

"Yeah, the 1st seems clear."

"We takin' the other stairs then."

"Anyone seen John and Shawn?" Ryan asked.

"No, man, they must be up already. We gonn' see them there."

And they once again split. It felt like one of those difficult level video games, that upper you go, the harder it gets. And they all were completely aware that it was not going to be easy.

In the meantime one of the children, a little girl, started crying.

"Melanie? What's wrong sweetheart?"

"I want to go the bathroom…" she cried.

"Honey…" Miss Smith hesitated "We can't leave the room now…"

"But I want to pee-pee so bad…" the little girl kept crying, putting the teacher in a very difficult situation.

"Ugh, honey… the bad dogs are outside…"

"But I want to…" the girl started crying louder.

"OK, sweetheart, we gonna go to the bathroom, but you have to keep quiet, OK? You mustn't cry, OK?"

"Okay…" the little girl whispered trying to hold it back.

The teacher got next to the door and put her ear on the door in an attempt to hear whether there were any dogs there.

"Honey, are you sure you can't keep it a few more minutes?" Miss Smith was really concerned.

"I'm suuure…" said the crying girl getting louder and jumping from one foot on the other.

"OK, Melanie, come here…" she grabbed her hand and turned to the class. "Kids, me and Melanie will now leave for a few seconds, but you stay here, and lock the door after I leave." And then turning towards the tallest kid "Sammy, I leave it on you, after I leave, you lock the door, and don't open it unless I say to, OK?"

"Okay, Miss Smith."

"Sammy, is that clear? I want you to close the door and stay here."

"Okay, Miss Smith, I got that, you can go."

"Thank you, honey, please take care…"

And she slowly grabbed the door handle when a series of 6 shots in a row was heard, and she cried out of reflex. The children got scared.

"It's okay, dears, remember the shots are coming from the good boy, right? Now you stay here, and Sammy, as I told you, okay?"

"Okay, Miss Smith…" the boy kept repeating.

For the second time the teacher grabbed the door handle, and this time she slowly pushed open the door that make a slight squeak. Holding tight onto Melanie's hand, she left the room, and once again signaled at Sammy to close the door and lock it. As she left, the little boy quickly locked the door.

"She's gonna be back, right Sammy?" one of the little girls asked.

"I am sure she will." He said, being probably the calmest kid form the entire group.

In the corridor Miss Smith could hear whispers coming from the 2nd floor, the Hood's Brothers were near, she felt a bit safe, and as she wanted to open the bathroom's door, that was facing the room's door, a huge pit-bull came out of it. The little girl peed herself at the sight of the massive and horrifying dog, while the teacher froze holding tight on the little girl's hand. The dog looked tense, his teeth shown and ready to growl. His sharp teeth and muzzle were covered in blood, and so was his chest. The little girl was shaking terribly. The teacher couldn't move either. As the bathroom door cracked open, Melanie and Miss Smith could see the mutilated body of their janitor. It was a horrifying scene. The girl could barely hold her tears back. Just as the dog starting growling louder, a loud shot filled the air, and the dog feel down. It was Frank. He arrived just in time to shoot the raging dog and save both the teacher and the little girl.

"Oh gosh, we are so thankful!" the teacher burst into tears.

"It's all fine now, it's all good, the dogs are gonne now."

But just as he managed to say the word, they heart cries coming from the second floor.

"Michael?!" Frank shouted, then turning to the teacher "Get in there now, and don't open until I say so!"

Miss Smith grabbed the girl and got inside the room, while Frank run to the 2nd floor. There Michael was downs on the floor with his leg bleeding, while Tony, Shawn, and the other guys were beating the last pit-bull with their baseball bats.

"Fuck! That bastard bit you!" frank exclaimed.

"Nah, I'm good, homie, when I have kids Imma be a hero…" he laughed, but his forehead was all covered in sweat.

"Oh, fuck…" Scot whispered.

"What?!"

"The dogs have rabies…" he whispered do that only Frank hear him.

"Oh, Fuck…" Frank gasped. "Scot, grab Shawn, and go to the hospital, now!"

"Wha', nigga, I need no hospital…" Michael made an effort to raise on his elbows.

"You goin' to the hospital, they gotta clean yo wound, Scot."

Shawn and Scot grabbed Michael and helped him up. They went to the car and headed straight to the nearest hospital, that was around 1 hour of driving away.

"Throw this fucker somewhere, I don't want the kids seeing it when they get down." Frank threw a kick in the dead pit-bull and went upstairs. When he got in the room the teacher and the children cheered him and run towards him hugging him.

"We are so grateful…" the teacher whispered through tears.

"Sammy said you are Katie's brother, is it true?" a little girl dared to ask.

"Yeah, that's truth, I only came because she said I must come save you!" he smiled back at the kids.

"You better call the police, miss, someone needs to clean all this mess, and those bastards are no better than any trash-men…" the teacher could hear on Frank's voice that he was really pissed on the authorities.

"Thank you once again… Frank…" Miss smith dared say as she slightly blushed.

Chapter 7

"Scot, you motherfucker, you got the best memory out of this!" Frank said as he entered the hospital room Scot was it. He right leg was all in gypsum, apparently the wild pit-bull crippled his entire bone.

"Told ya mah kids gonna be proud." And he laughed.

Soon after, the other homies got in, too.

"An' here we have the toughest nigga of them all!" Ryan said "I was there! I saw it all!" and he pointed at himself with pride.

"Yeah, man, that was wild." Michael said.

"Id' do it any day again…" Tony shook his head.

"Martin is now revenged." Frank patted him on the shoulder.

"We gotta get drunk, yo! Tears are for the pussies!" Scot shouted as he sensed Tony get emotional. "Bet Martin is now blowing smoke and restin' his feet on a leather couch with Jesus."

"Man, he was wild, wish he saw you with gypsum, he'd laugh his ass off." Frank gasped.

A few minutes later the door opened, and Miss Smith came in to see the wounded. Ryan couldn't help but whistle at her as Frank gave him an elbow.

"I couldn't be more grateful what you did for us, guys." She said with compassion.

"Tell that to our brother Scot, he felt it better, ha-ha!" John laughed.

"We really are grateful…" she said as she turned her head towards the door continuing "Kids?"

The door opened wide and a dozen of children burst in holding each a drawing of the good boys beating the bad dogs. Katie was the first to come in and she run straight up to Frank, jumped into his arms, and yelled. "I knew you'd save them! I knew you'd beat the bad dogs' asses!"

Frank covered her little mouth being embarrassed, while everyone laughed.

"Shhh, Katie, you can't say that…"

"But you always say it, Frank! You also say 'fuck them bastards!'" and she tried to make an impression of Frank's angry voice. Perhaps it was one of the most embarrassing moment frank has ever lived through.

"You're my hero!" a little girl went to Scot's bed handing him a drawing. It was a terrible drawing, but Scot loved it, because it was showing him beating a dog with a bloody baseball bat.

"Cool baseball you drew, lil' one!"

"Nooo, it's not a baseball! I's your broken leg! You took it and beat the bad dog with it!" the little girl said enthusiastic, and everyone burst into laughter.

"Guys, turn on the news!" a nurse run in shouting. Tony turned the TV on, and there was the news.

"..luckily, the Hood's Brothers made it in time to save the 28 children and the teacher trapped at the 3rd floor." Said the reporter.

"We are really thankful for having such responsible citizens that decided to give a helping hand in need." Were the words of the officer representative.

"Yeah, fuckers, keep talking…" Shawn mumbled, realizing he was surrounded by kids, while the nurse gave him an elbow.

About an hour later everyone left, the only people around were Scot, obviously, Frank, Katie, and Miss Smith, who for some reason didn't want to leave.

"It's about time you leave, too, homie. Thanks for bein' here." Scot finally said.

"Yeah, get well soon!"

"Get well soon, Scot! Frank says you're a badass!" Katie said.

"Katie…" Frank gave her the look.

As they left the hospital, it was dark already.

"Maybe we should walk home Miss Smith first." Katie said grinning.

"Oh, why, no, it's OK…" Miss Smith blushed.

"Or maybe we should leave you home first." Frank looked at the young teacher while petting Katie's head.

"Maybe!" Katie giggled.

"Sorry, she knows way too much for her age…" Frank apologized embarrassed.

"It's OK." She shyly lowered her head smiling.

They all got into the car and headed towards Frank's house.

"Will you come in for a drink?"

"I don't see why not." She replied.

"Wooooooh!" Katie exclaimed.

"Katie! Be polite!" and they both laughed.

They got in for a drink, but it all obviously turned out to be more than a drink…

CPSIA information can be obtained at www.ICGtesting.com
Printed in the USA
LVOW10s1021010716

PP11077600001B/4/P